For my grandmother, Sophia Morton – F.H.

LADYBIRD BOOKS, INC.
Auburn, Maine 04210 U.S.A.
© LADYBIRD BOOKS LTD 1990
Loughborough, Leicestershire, England

All rights reserved. No part of this publication may be reproduced, stored in a retrieval system, or transmitted in any form or by any means, electronic, mechanical, photocopying, recording or otherwise, without the prior consent of the copyright owner.

Printed in England

The Ten Commandments

Retold by Fern Howard
Illustrated by Barbara Steadman

Ladybird Books

For many years the people of Israel had been slaves in Egypt. The cruel Pharaoh, ruler of Egypt, made the Israelites work hard night and day. He would not even let them take time to worship the Lord.

One day, God told Moses it was time to lead the Israelites out of Egypt. After many struggles, Pharaoh released them, and they followed Moses into the wilderness to begin the journey to the land God had promised them.

It took forty years to walk from Egypt to the Promised Land. Sometimes the people thought they would not have enough food or water or protection from the heat, but the Lord always gave them whatever they needed.

Every morning a delicious food called manna appeared on the ground, so the people always had enough to eat. In the desert the Lord made water spring from a rock, so the people were never thirsty.

God told Moses that he wanted the Israelites to obey certain laws. "If you obey my laws," God said, "you will be my special treasure. You shall be a holy nation." God told Moses to bring the people to Mount Sinai.

Moses led the people to the foot of the mountain. Smoke billowed into the sky as God came down, and the whole mountain shook with a mighty earthquake.

Then God called Moses to the top of the mountain. He gave Moses ten laws, called commandments, for the people who served him to obey.

These are the ten commandments the Lord gave to Moses:

I am the Lord your God, who released you when you were slaves in Egypt. Worship no other god but me.

Keep the Sabbath as a holy day. Six days a week are for work, but the seventh day is a day of rest.

For in six days, God made the world, and he rested on the seventh, so he made the Sabbath and set it aside for rest.

Respect your father and your mother.

When God had finished speaking, he gave Moses two tablets of stone, on which he had written these Ten Commandments.

Moses came down from the mountain and told the people what God had said. And the Israelites saw lightning and smoke and thunderclouds billowing up from the mountain, and they shook with fear.

Moses said, "Do not be afraid. God shows his power so you will obey."

Then the people remembered God's promise to love those who obeyed his commandments, so they weren't afraid. They told Moses, "We will obey them all."